For Ned W.   P.H.
For Dorothy   K.D.

First published 1987 by Walker Books Ltd
184-192 Drummond Street, London NW1 3HP

Text © 1987 Pamela Zinnemann-Hope
Illustrations © 1987 Kady MacDonald Denton

First printed 1987
Printed and bound by L.E.G.O., Vicenza, Italy

British Library Cataloguing in Publication Data
Zinnemann-Hope, Pamela
Let's play ball Ned
I. Title   II. Denton, Kady MacDonald
823'.914 [J]   PZ7

ISBN 0-7445-0628-X

Let's play ball
NED

Written by Pam Zinnemann-Hope

Illustrated by Kady MacDonald Denton

WALKER BOOKS
LONDON

"Dad, what can I play?"

"Why not play with
Fred today?"

"Fred, where's the ball?"

"Let's play ball."

"Shhh, Fred."

"Fetch, Fred."

"Dad, did you call?"

"Oh, Fred!"

"Ned. Look at the hall!
Look at it all!"

"I'm sorry, Dad."

"Let's tidy the hall."

"I'll wipe the wall."

"I'll hide the ball."

"Let's go outside."

"Let's all play ball."

"Catch, Ned."